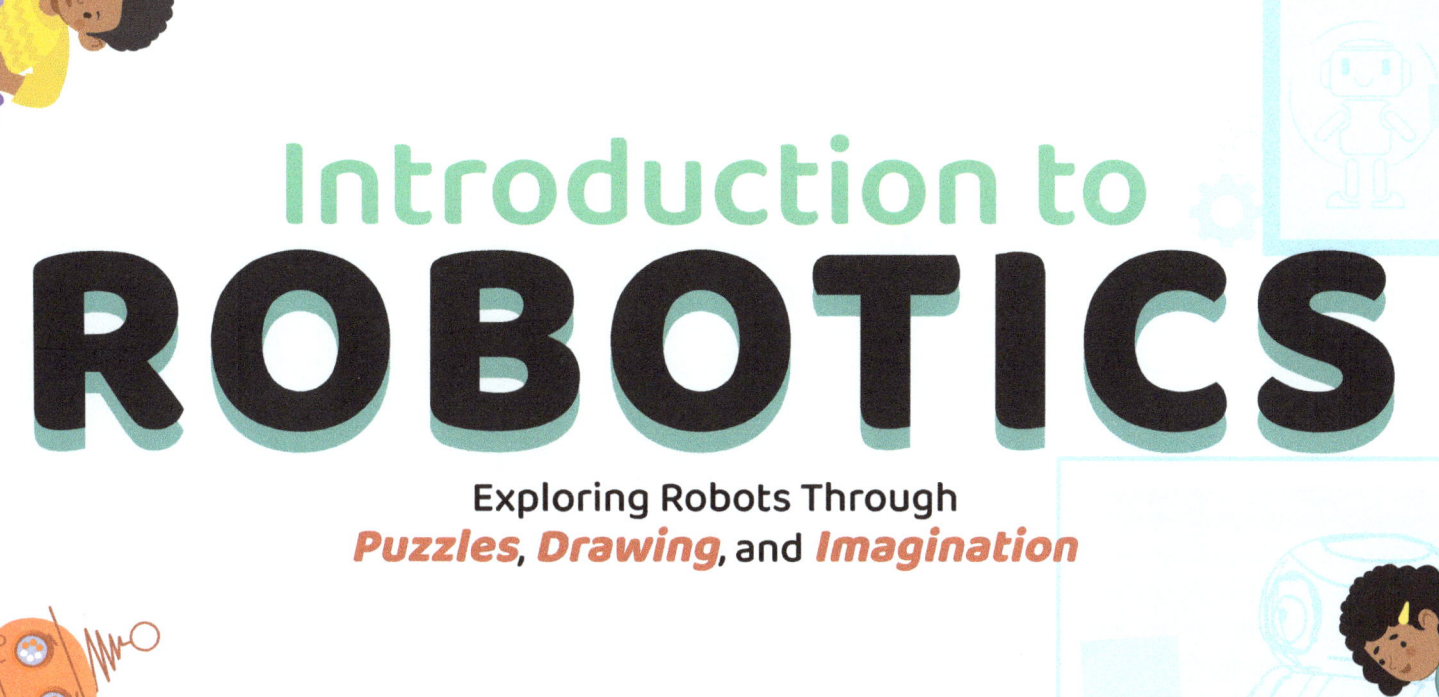

Introduction to ROBOTICS

Exploring Robots Through *Puzzles*, *Drawing*, and *Imagination*

MOONSTONE

Published in Moonstone
by Rupa Publications India Pvt. Ltd 2025
7/16, Ansari Road, Daryaganj
New Delhi 110002

Sales centres:
Bengaluru Chennai
Hyderabad Jaipur Kathmandu
Kolkata Mumbai Prayagraj

Copyright © Rupa Publications India Pvt. Ltd 2025

All rights reserved.

No part of this publication may be reproduced, transmitted,
or stored in a retrieval system, in any form or by any means,
electronic, mechanical, photocopying, recording or otherwise,
without the prior permission of the publisher.

P-ISBN: 978-93-6156-905-0
E-ISBN: 978-93-6156-631-8

First impression 2025

10 9 8 7 6 5 4 3 2 1

Printed in India
This book is sold subject to the condition that it shall not,
by way of trade or otherwise, be lent, resold, hired out, or otherwise
circulated, without the publisher's prior consent, in any form of binding
or cover other than that in which it is published.

Chapter 1
What Are Robots?

Robots are special machines that follow instructions to do tasks. But what makes something a robot?

Here's what defines a robot:

1. **Sensors:** Robots use sensors to detect their surroundings. For example, a robot vacuum has sensors to avoid bumping into walls.

2. **Brain (Program):** Robots have a computer that tells them what to do. This is called programming.

3. **Moving Parts:** Robots use wheels, arms, or legs to perform actions like rolling, picking, or walking.

Robots can look different. Some look like people, others like animals, and many just look like machines. For example:

- A robot vacuum cleans floors.
- A toy robot can talk or move.
- A factory robot builds cars or machines.

Fun Fact: The word "robot" comes from a Czech word meaning "work" or "labor."

Activities

1. **Match the Robot to Its Job**

Vacuum Robot	Builds cars
Toy Robot	Cleans the floor
Factory Robot	Talks and moves for fun

2. **Robot Parts**
Fill in the blanks.

1. Robots use _____ to sense their surroundings.

2. The _____ tells a robot what to do.

3. Robots use _____ to move and complete tasks.

3. **Draw Your Helper Robot**
Design a robot that helps you at school or home. What does it look like? What job does it do? Write one sentence about it.

_____

Chapter 2
The History of Robots

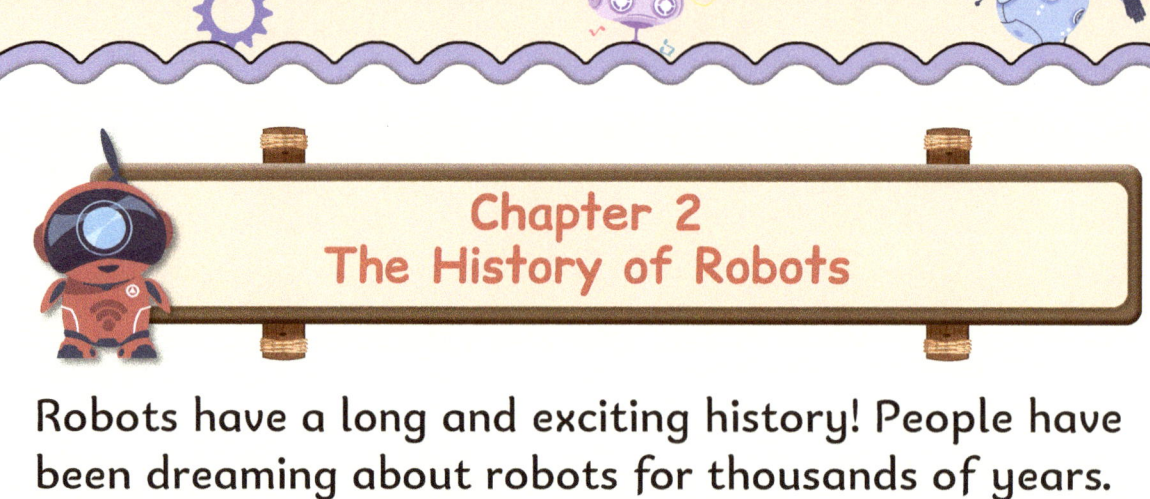

Robots have a long and exciting history! People have been dreaming about robots for thousands of years.

- **Ancient Times:** Simple machines like water clocks were invented to work on their own. These were the earliest "robotic" ideas.

- **1400s:** Leonardo da Vinci created designs for a mechanical knight that could sit, wave, and move its head.

- **1920s:** The word "robot" was first used in a play called R.U.R. by Karel Čapek.

- **1950s:** Real robots were built for factories to lift and assemble heavy objects.

- **Today:** Robots explore space, perform surgeries, and even act as companions for people.

Fun Fact: Robots can be as small as a bug or as big as a building crane!

Activities

1. **Timeline Sorting**
   Rearrange these events in the correct order:
   1. Robots were used in factories.
   2. The word "robot" was first used in a play.
   3. Leonardo da Vinci designed a mechanical knight.

2. **Fill in the Blanks**
   1. The word "robot" was first used in the play _____.
   2. Robots were first used in _____ to lift and assemble things.
   3. Leonardo da Vinci designed a mechanical _____.

3. **Design a Historic Robot**
   Imagine you're an inventor in the 1400s. What kind of robot would you build, and what job would it do? Draw it and name it!

Chapter 3
Famous Robots Around Us

Robots are everywhere, helping us in amazing ways. Here are some famous real-life robots and what they do:

- **Sofia:** A humanoid robot with a human-like face. Sofia can talk, show emotions, and even crack jokes! She's like a robot celebrity, appearing on TV shows and interviews.

- **Spot:** This robot dog from Boston Dynamics can run, climb stairs, and even carry heavy things. It's used for exploring dangerous places where humans can't go.

- **Roomba:** A small, round robot that cleans your house while you relax. It moves around, sweeping up dirt and dust on its own.

- **Curiosity:** A space robot that's been on Mars for over 10 years, taking pictures and sending information back to Earth.

- **Asimo:** A walking robot by Honda. Asimo can walk, run, and even serve drinks!

Fun Fact: Robots like Curiosity are called "rovers," and they explore planets that humans can't visit yet.

Activities

1. Match the Robot to Its Job

Draw lines to match the robot with its description.

Robot	Job
Sofia	A humanoid robot that talks and cracks jokes
Spot	A robot dog that carries heavy loads
Roomba	A robot vacuum that cleans houses
Curiosity	A rover exploring Mars
Asimo	A walking robot that serves drinks

2. Fill in the Blanks

Complete the sentences using the words in the box.

Words: Sofia, Spot, Roomba, Curiosity, Asimo

1. The robot that explores Mars is called _____.

2. _____ is a robot dog that can carry heavy loads.

3. _____ is famous for walking and serving drinks.

4. _____ cleans houses without any help.

5. A robot celebrity that talks and jokes is named _____.

Chapter 4
Robots in Movies and Stories

Robots have been a big part of stories and movies for a long time. They often have super cool features and abilities, and some even become our best friends! Here are some famous robots from movies and stories:

- **R2-D2 (Star Wars):** This little droid may be small, but he's mighty! R2-D2 is a trusty helper to the heroes of the Star Wars universe. He can fix things, carry messages, and even save the day with his quick thinking.

- **WALL-E (WALL-E):** WALL-E is a cute robot who spends his days cleaning up Earth after humans have left. He's curious and friendly, and even falls in love with another robot named Eve.

- **Bumblebee (Transformers):** Bumblebee is a car that can turn into a robot! He's part of a group of robots called the Autobots, who fight to protect Earth from evil robots.

- **The Iron Giant (The Iron Giant):** This huge robot is friendly and wants to protect a young boy from danger. Even though he's big and strong, he's kind-hearted and brave.

- **C-3PO (Star Wars):** A golden humanoid robot, C-3PO is fluent in over six million forms of communication! He's always there to help his friends, even though he's often nervous.

> **Fun Fact:** Some of the robots in stories and movies are inspired by real robots, while others are completely imagined to be super powerful or even magical!

Activities

1. **Match the Robot to Its Movie**

Draw lines to match the robot with the movie or story.

Robot	Movie/Story
R2-D2	The Iron Giant
WALL-E	Transformers
Bumblebee	Star Wars
The Iron Giant	WALL-E
C-3PO	Transformers

2. **Fill in the Blanks**

Complete the sentences using the words in the box.

1. _____ is a robot that loves to clean Earth and finds a friend in Eve.

2. The robot that can turn into a car is called _____.

3. _____ helps the Star Wars heroes and is great at fixing things.

4. _____ is a huge robot with a kind heart who protects a young boy.

5. _____ is a golden robot who can speak many languages.

3. **Which Robot Are You Most Like?**
Draw a picture of yourself, and add a robot character next to you that you think you're most like. Is it R2-D2, WALL-E, or maybe C-3PO? What qualities do you share with that robot?

_____

_____

Chapter 5
How Robots Work

Robots might seem like magic, but they actually work with a few simple things: sensors, motors, and commands. Let's break it down:

- **Sensors:** Sensors are like the robot's senses. They help the robot "see" and "feel" the world around it. For example, a robot might have a sensor to detect when it bumps into something or when there is an object in its way. It's like how we use our eyes and hands to feel things!

- **Motors:** Motors are like the muscles of the robot. They make the robot move! Whether it's moving wheels, arms, or legs, motors are responsible for the action.

- **Commands:** Commands are instructions telling the robot what to do. These instructions come from a programmer or a computer and guide the robot through its tasks. It's like giving directions to a friend – "Go straight, turn left, pick up the ball!"

Think of a robot as a mix of eyes (sensors), muscles (motors), and a brain (commands)!

Activities

1. **Label the Robot Parts**

Draw lines to connect the robot parts with their function.

Robot Part	Function
Sensors	Help the robot see and feel its surroundings
Motors	Make the robot move
Commands	Tell the robot what to do

2. **What's Inside the Robot?**

Fill in the blanks to complete the sentences.

1. Robots use _____ to see and feel their surroundings.

2. The _____ makes the robot move around and do tasks.

3. A _____ gives the robot instructions on what to do.

3. Draw a Robot's Senses

Imagine a robot that uses all five senses like a human! Draw a robot with eyes (sensors), arms (motors), and a brain (commands). What can it do? Draw it in action!

_____

_____

Chapter 6
Robots That Help Us

Robots are not just for fun! Many robots help us in real life. Here are some examples:

- **Home Robots:** These are robots that help with housework. For example, Roomba is a robot vacuum that cleans the floor by itself!

- **Hospital Robots:** In hospitals, robots can help doctors with surgery or even deliver medicine. Da Vinci Surgical System is a robot that helps surgeons perform precise operations.

- **Factory Robots:** In factories, robots help build things like cars. They work with great speed and accuracy to make production faster.

- **Rescue Robots:** There are robots used to help during emergencies, like searching for people after a disaster. They can go places that are too dangerous for people to go.

Robots make life easier and help us do things faster, safer, and more efficiently!

Activities

1. **Symmetrical Drawing**

Complete the picture and color it.

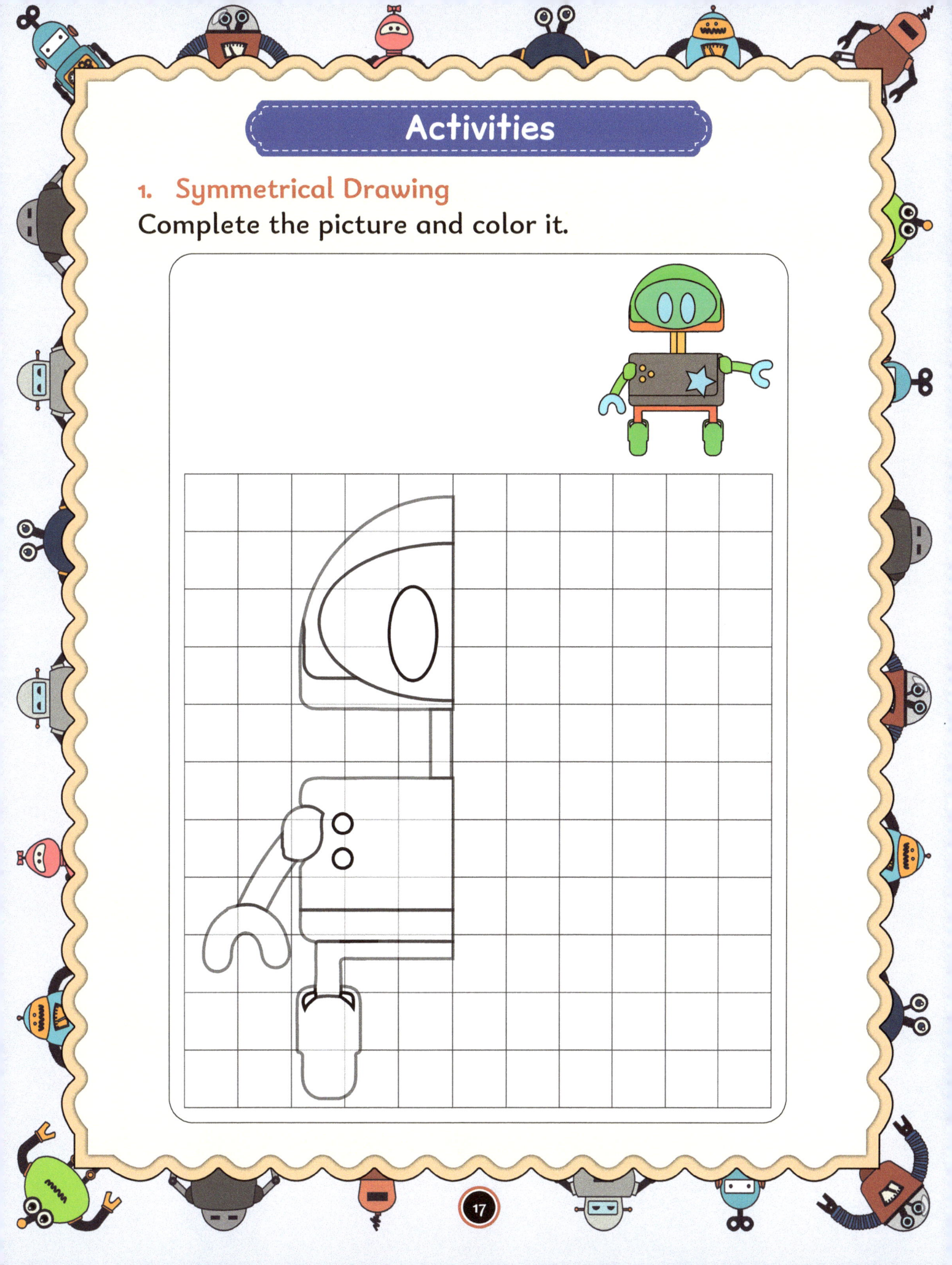

2. **Where Would You Use a Robot?**
Think of a place where robots could help you. It could be at home, in a hospital, or even in space! Draw a picture of the robot and what it's doing to help.

3. **Fill in the Blanks**
Fill in the blanks with the correct answers.

1. The robot that helps clean the house is called _____.

2. _____ robots help doctors perform surgery with precision.

3. Robots in factories help build _____.

4. _____ robots are used to search for people after disasters.

Chapter 7
Animal-Inspired Robots

Did you know that some robots are inspired by animals? Engineers and designers look at how animals move, hunt, or fly, and then create robots that work in a similar way!

- **Robotic Fish:** Engineers have made fish-like robots that swim through water just like real fish. These robots are used for exploring oceans or cleaning underwater places.

- **Robotic Birds:** Some robots are designed to fly like birds. They are light, flexible, and can soar through the air.

- **Robotic Insects:** Tiny robots are made to look like insects. For example, robots that fly like bees or crawl like ants! These robots can help in places where humans can't go, like inside pipes or small spaces.

- **Robotic Dogs:** Some robots look like dogs and are designed to help in rescue missions. These robots can climb stairs and help find people who are lost!

Animals have inspired some of the most amazing robots, showing that nature has some brilliant ideas!

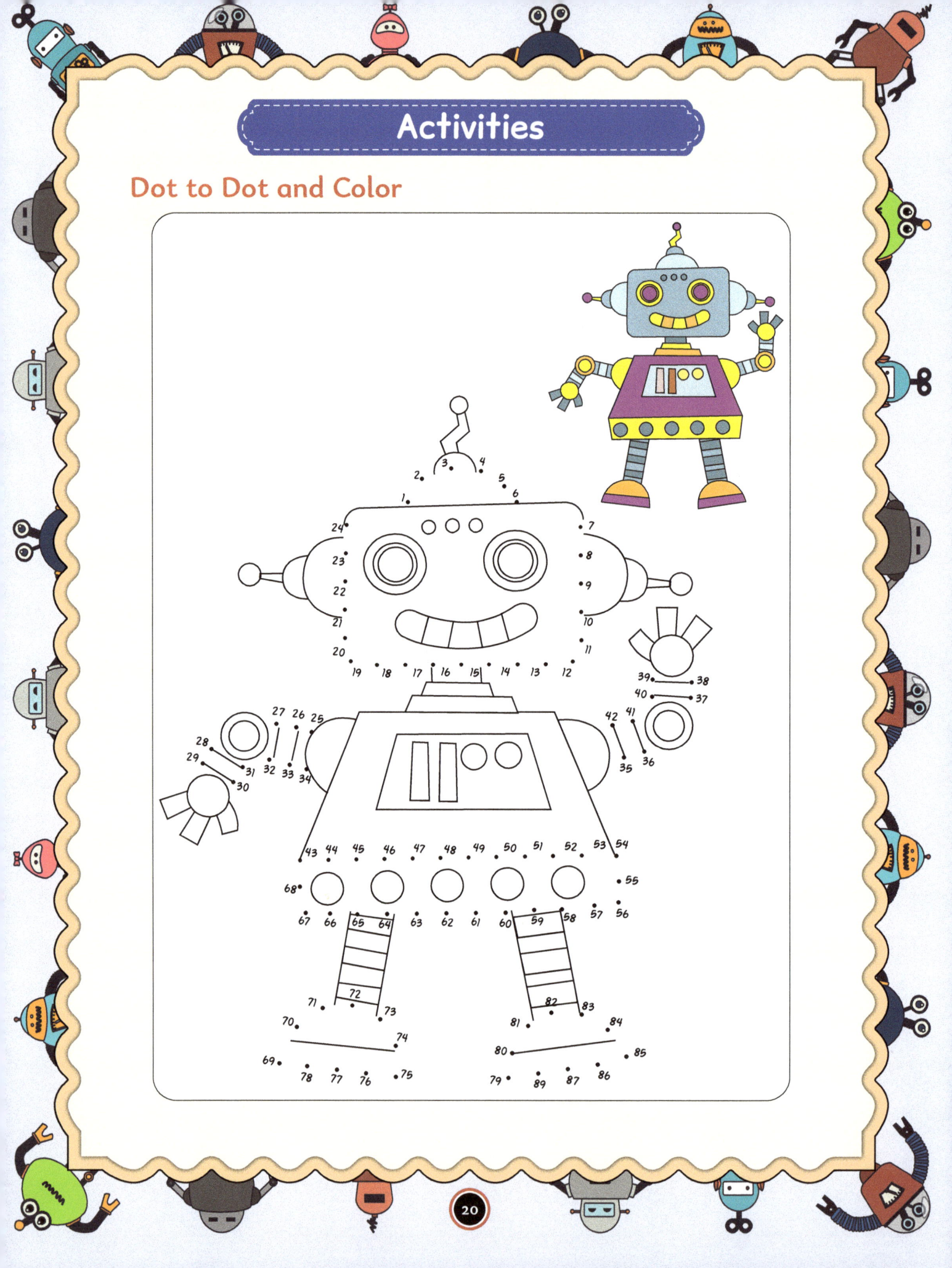

Chapter 8
Robot Facts

Ready to be amazed by some fun robot facts? Here are some cool things about robots that will blow your mind!

- **Robots Can Have Superhuman Strength:** Some robots are designed to lift heavy things. In factories, robots can lift objects that are way too heavy for humans!

- **The First Robot Was Created in 1495:** The first robot-like machine was created by Leonardo da Vinci. It was a mechanical knight that could sit, wave its arms, and move its head.

- **There Are Robots That Can Paint:** Some robots can paint pictures! These robots use sensors to pick the perfect colors and create art just like humans.

- **Robots Can Learn:** Some robots can even "learn" by practicing tasks over and over, just like how we get better at playing games or sports!

- **Robots in Space:** NASA uses robots to explore planets and moons. Some robots help astronauts by fixing spacecraft and doing experiments in space!

Activities

1. Robot Word Search

Find these words hidden in the grid:

- Strength
- Da Vinci
- Learn
- Paint
- Space

P	A	I	N	T	X	M	F	D
I	J	K	M	N	I	V	O	T
H	W	O	Z	X	C	L	O	M
T	R	E	I	H	I	B	P	A
L	S	Q	S	P	C	M	D	X
E	I	C	O	D	P	R	H	L
A	S	B	T	A	V	I	N	C
R	U	D	O	C	I	E	N	A

2. Robot Fun Fact Match-Up

Match the robot fun fact to the correct description.

Robot Fun Fact	Description
Robots Can Learn	Some robots can create art
The First Robot Was Created by Da Vinci	Robots can lift objects heavier than humans
Robots Can Paint	NASA uses robots to explore space

3. True or False?

Read the statements and circle if they are True or False.

1. Robots can lift heavy objects. (True / False)
2. The first robot was made in 2000. (True / False)
3. Some robots can paint pictures. (True / False)
4. Robots can't learn new things. (True / False)
5. NASA uses robots in space. (True / False)

Chapter 9
Robots Around the World

Robots are used all over the world, and they help people in different ways. Let's take a look at how robots are being used in different countries!

- **Japan:** Japan is known for its robots! They use robots in factories to build cars and electronics. Japan also has robots that entertain people, like robotic pets!

- **USA:** In the United States, robots are used in hospitals to help doctors perform surgery. They also help astronauts explore space.

- **Europe:** In Europe, robots are used in agriculture. They help farmers by planting seeds, watering crops, and even picking fruits.

- **China:** China is using robots in many factories to make things faster and safer. They also use robots to help with construction projects!

- **India:** In India, robots are being used in healthcare to assist doctors and provide treatment for patients.

Robots help people everywhere by making jobs easier, faster, and safer.

Activities

1. Robot Country Match-Up

Match the country to the robot job it is known for.

Country	Robot Job
Japan	Robots in healthcare
USA	Robots in factories and space exploration
Europe	Robots in agriculture
China	Robots in construction and factories
India	Robots in healthcare and assistance

2. Color the Astronaut Robot

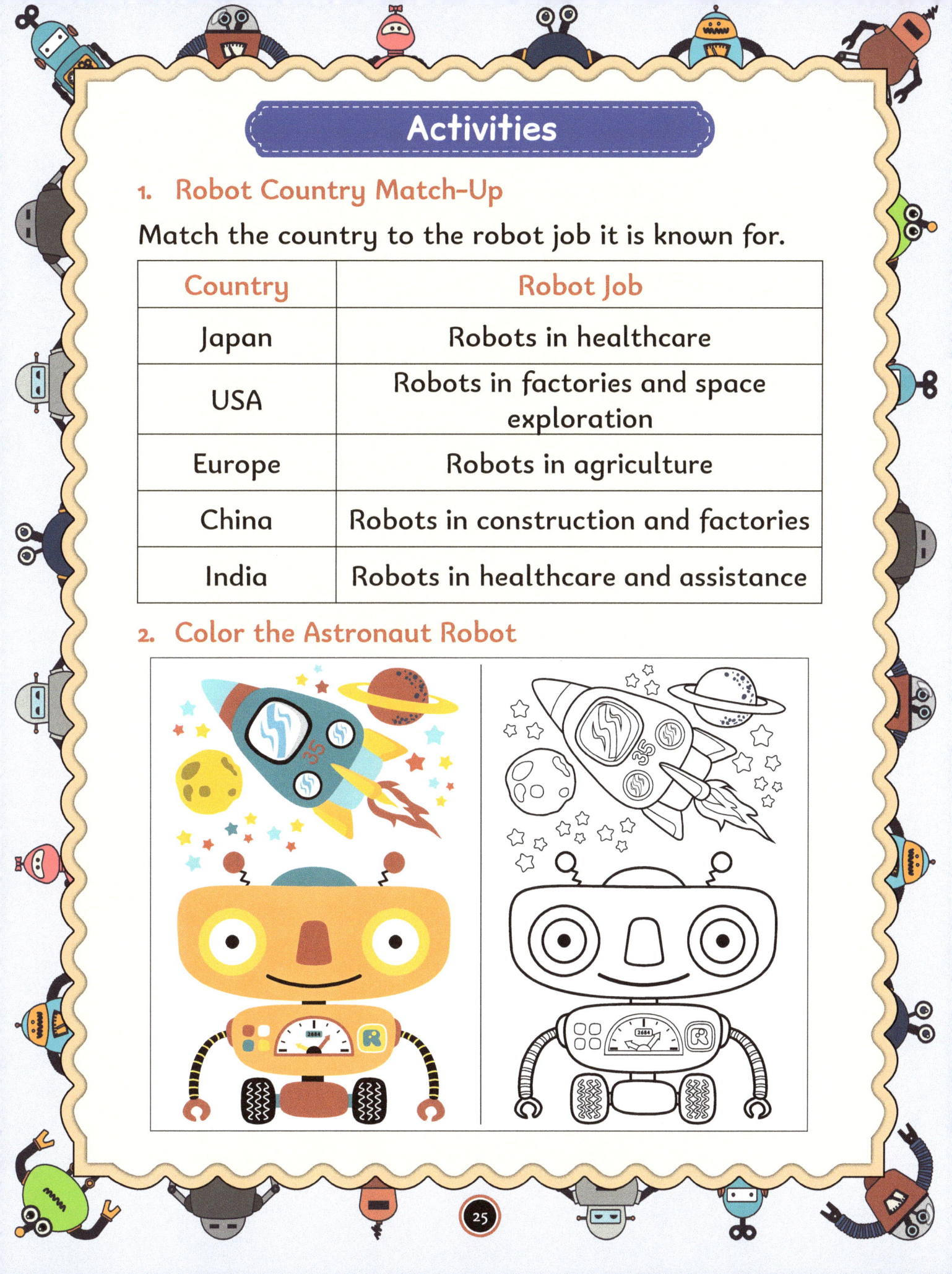

Chapter 10
How Robots See the World

How do robots "see" the world around them? They use special tools like sensors and cameras to understand what's happening around them!

- **Sensors:** These are like robot "eyes." Sensors can detect obstacles, changes in light, temperature, or even sound! For example, a robot vacuum uses sensors to find dirt on the floor and avoid obstacles like walls or furniture.

- **Cameras:** Robots can also have cameras that help them see and recognize objects. Some robots use cameras to detect faces or find their way around.

- **LIDAR:** LIDAR stands for "Light Detection and Ranging." It's a special tool that robots use to measure the distance to objects and help them understand their surroundings in 3D.

Sensors and cameras work together to help robots "see" and make smart decisions. Just like how our eyes help us navigate the world, robots use sensors to do the same!

Activities

Charge the Robot

Robin, the Robot, needs your help to reach the charged battery and start his daily chores. Help him.

Chapter 11
Design Your Dream Robot

Imagine a world where you can create a robot that can do anything! Designing robots is super fun because you can decide what your robot looks like and what it does. Let's think about what makes your robot special!

A robot needs three important things:

1. **Sensors:** These are like the robot's senses. It helps the robot see, hear, or feel things around it.
2. **Brains (Processor):** This is the robot's computer! It helps the robot think and make decisions.
3. **Actions:** The robot can move, talk, or do anything you tell it to.

Now that we know what robots need, let's imagine your dream robot!

- What will it look like? It could be a big walking robot, a small flying one, or something you've never seen before!
- What will it do? Does it help with schoolwork, clean your room, or even cook your dinner?
- What is its special power? Maybe your robot can talk to animals, fly, or even play music!

Designing a robot is all about creativity. The best part is you get to decide what your robot will do!

Activities

1. **Draw Your Robot**

   Draw your dream robot! Use the space below to design your robot and make it as cool as you want. Think about how it looks, what it can do, and what its superpower is.

2. **Describe Your Robot**

   Write down some fun details about your robot:
   - What is its name? _____
   - What can it do? _____
   - What makes it special? _____

Chapter 12
Robot Adventures

Robot Adventure Time!

Imagine you and your robot are on an adventure. Where are you going? What will you do? The great thing about robots is that they can help you on any adventure. Whether you're exploring a jungle, traveling to space, or solving mysteries, your robot is always there to help.

Here's how we can plan your robot adventure:

1. Where is the adventure? Maybe it's a jungle, a robot city, or a space station. Where do you want to go?

2. What is the goal? Are you looking for treasure, solving a mystery, or saving the day? Your robot can help you with the mission.

3. What obstacles will you face? Every adventure has challenges. Maybe you need to fix a broken bridge or fight off robots!

4. How does your robot help? Your robot can solve problems, build things, or fight bad guys. What can your robot do to help you finish the mission?

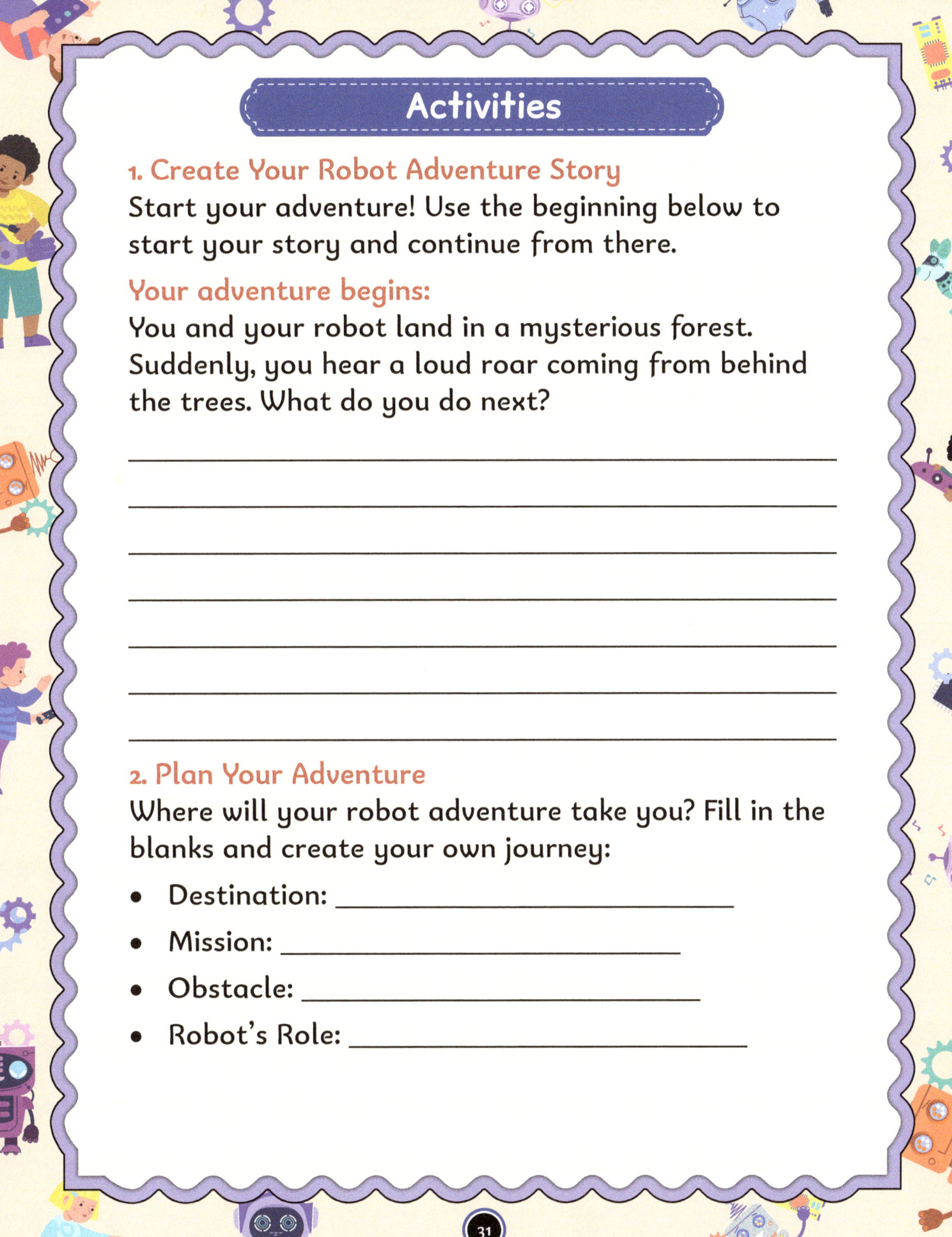

Activities

1. Create Your Robot Adventure Story

Start your adventure! Use the beginning below to start your story and continue from there.

Your adventure begins:
You and your robot land in a mysterious forest. Suddenly, you hear a loud roar coming from behind the trees. What do you do next?

_____
_____
_____
_____
_____
_____
_____
_____

2. Plan Your Adventure

Where will your robot adventure take you? Fill in the blanks and create your own journey:

- Destination: _____
- Mission: _____
- Obstacle: _____
- Robot's Role: _____

Chapter 13
Robots and Games

Robots and Games

Did you know robots can also be part of games? There are all kinds of toys, games, and even video games that feature robots. These robots can help you solve puzzles, play games, or even compete in races!

Types of Robot Games:

- **Robot Toys:** Some toys are robots that you can control with a remote or by programming them. They can walk, talk, or dance.

- **Robot Pets:** There are also robots that act like pets! These robot pets can bark, meow, or respond to you like a real pet.

- **Robot Video Games:** Many video games have robots that you control. You might be battling, racing, or solving puzzles with your robot team.

- **Robot Racing:** Some games have robot races, where robots race through obstacles and compete for the finish line.

Robots make games more fun because they're full of surprises, challenges, and tricks! Plus, you can even create your own robot game with your imagination.

How Many?

How many robots do you see?

Chapter 14
Robots in the Future

Robots are amazing right now, but just imagine what they could do in the future! The world of robotics is constantly changing, and we might see robots doing things that seem like science fiction today. Here are some ideas about what robots might be able to do in the future:

1. **Robot Doctors:** In the future, robots might help doctors by performing surgeries or checking your health. They could even make house calls to help you feel better.

2. **Robot Teachers:** Robots could become great teachers, helping kids learn all over the world! They might even teach you how to build robots.

3. **Robot Friends:** Imagine a robot that can talk to you, play games, and keep you company. These robots could be like best friends who never get tired!

4. **Robot Explorers:** Robots could help us explore space or even deep into the oceans. They could go places that are too dangerous for humans and bring back cool information.

The future is full of possibilities, and robots might do much more than we can imagine!

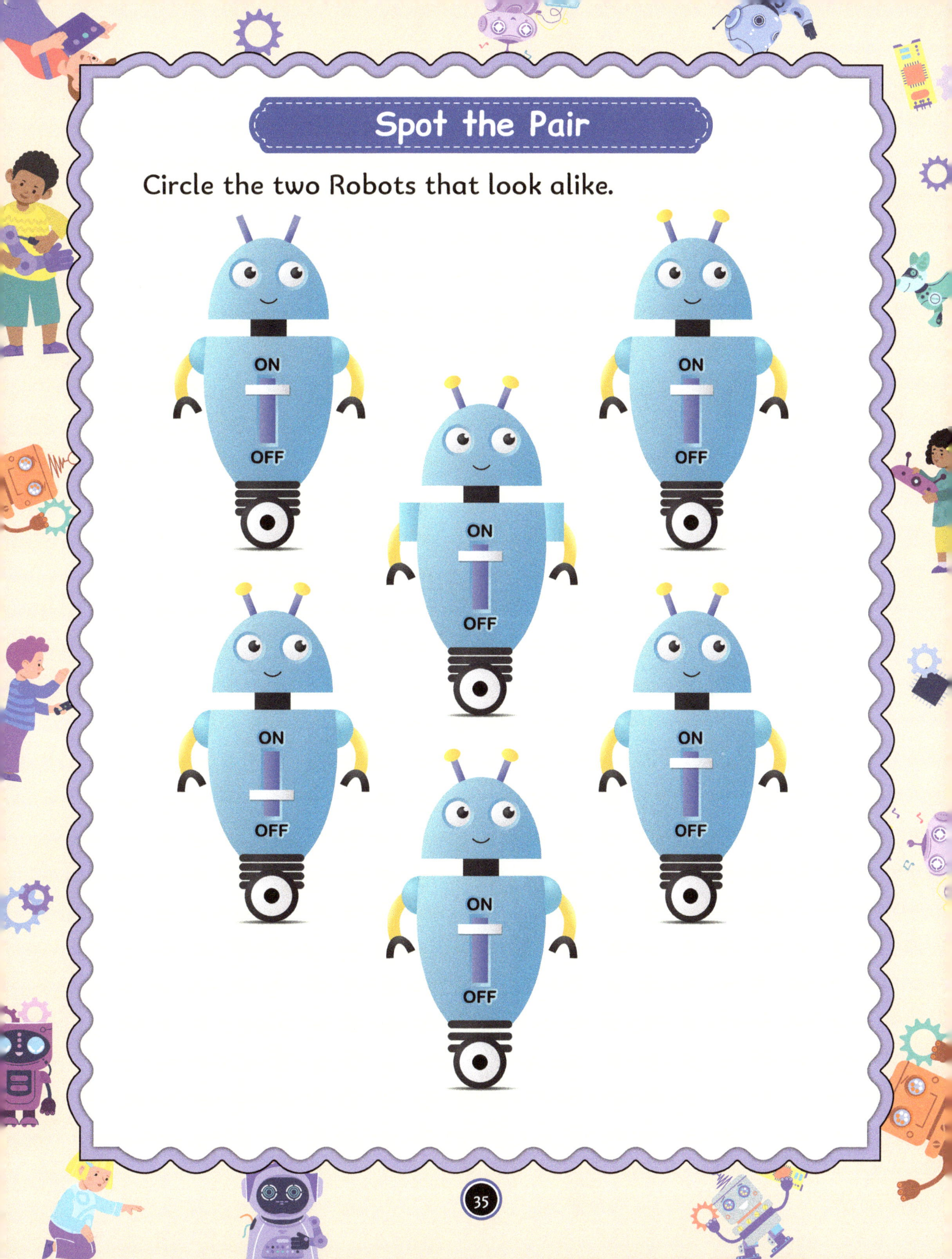

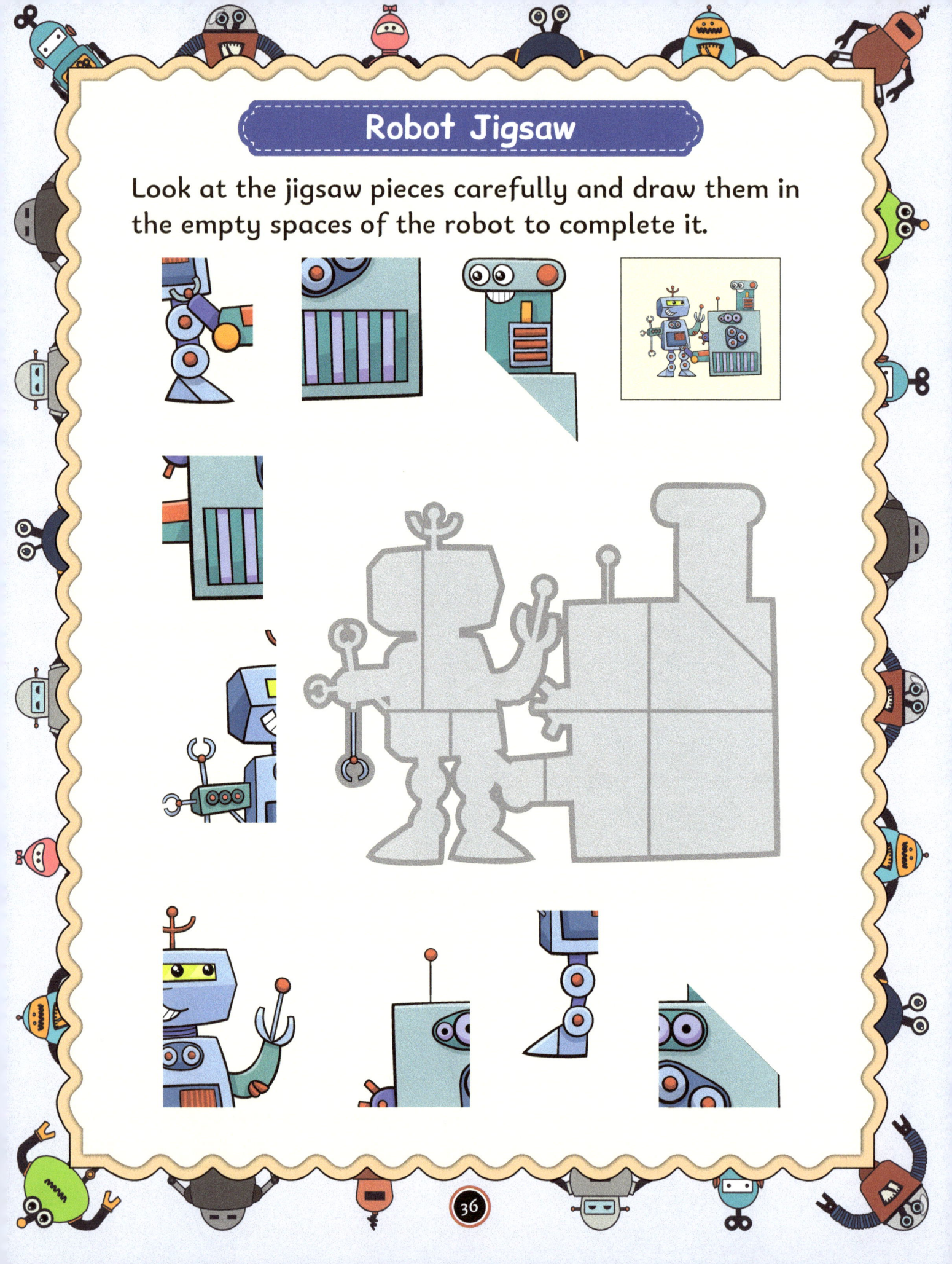

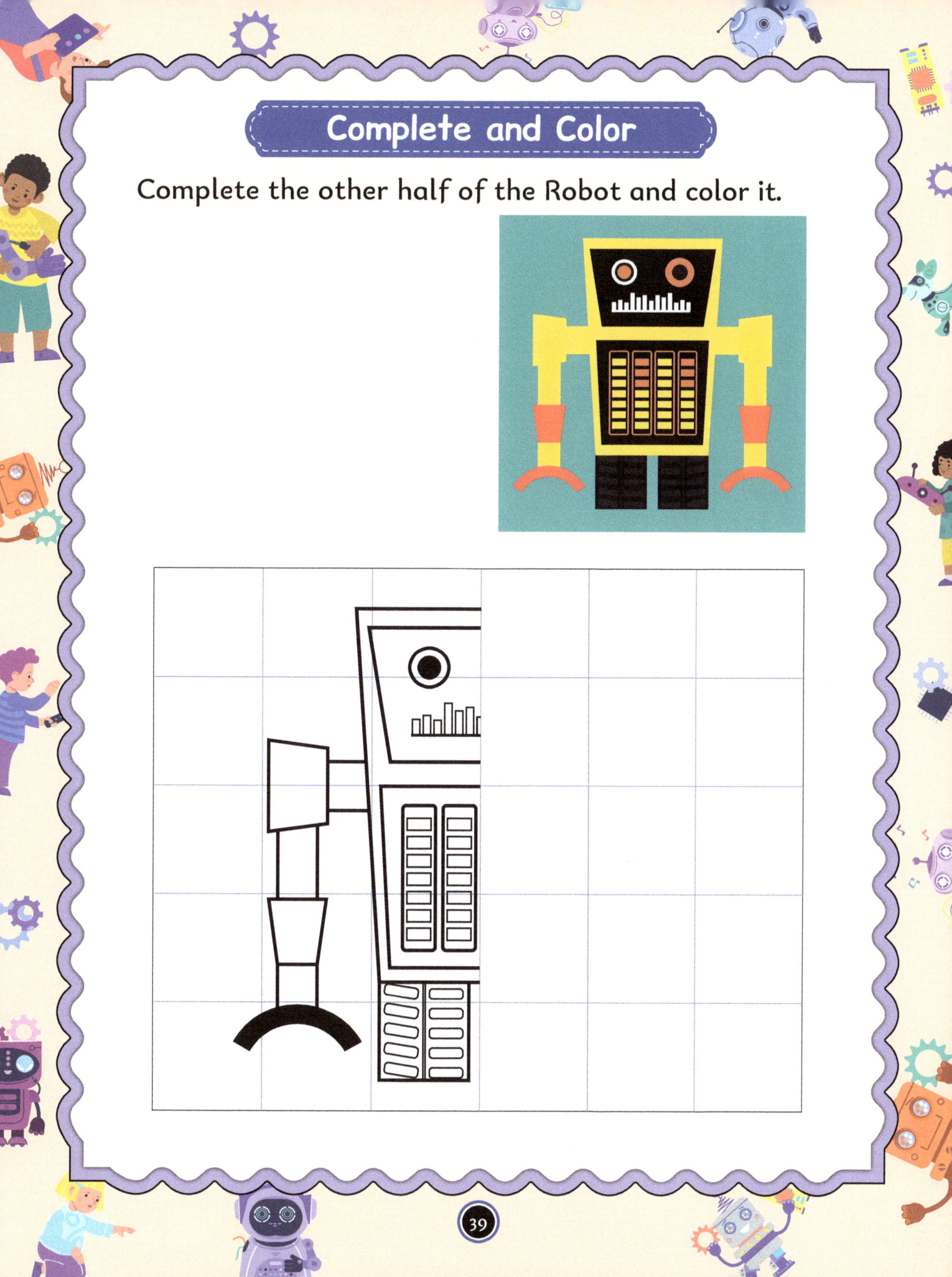

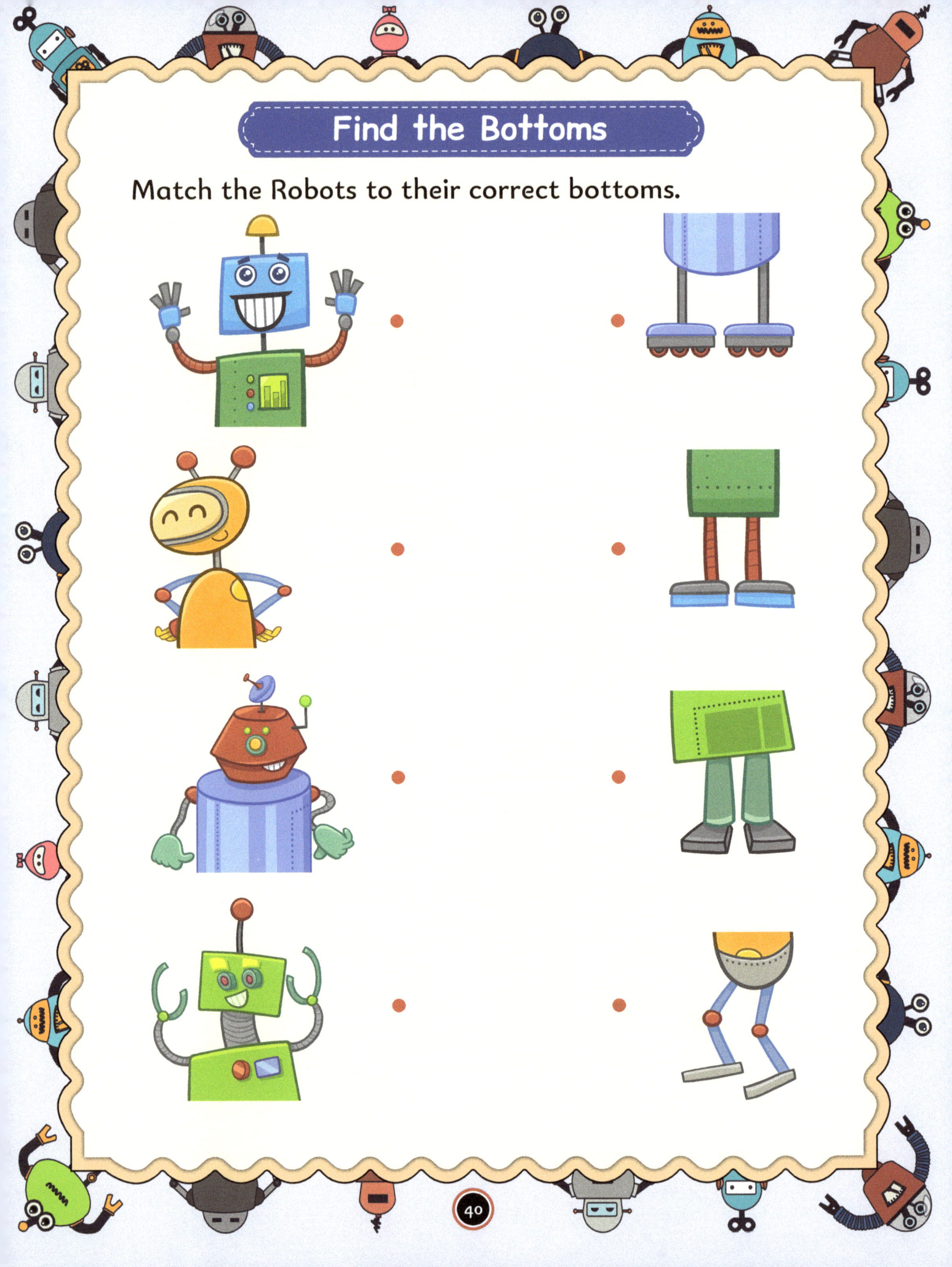

Math with Robots

Fill in the blanks to complete the sums.

1. 3 + ? = 8
   ? − 7 = 2

2. 4 + 5 = ?
   13 − ? = 8

3. ? + 10 = 15
   6 − ? = 0

Shadow Game

Pick the correct shadow that matches the image.

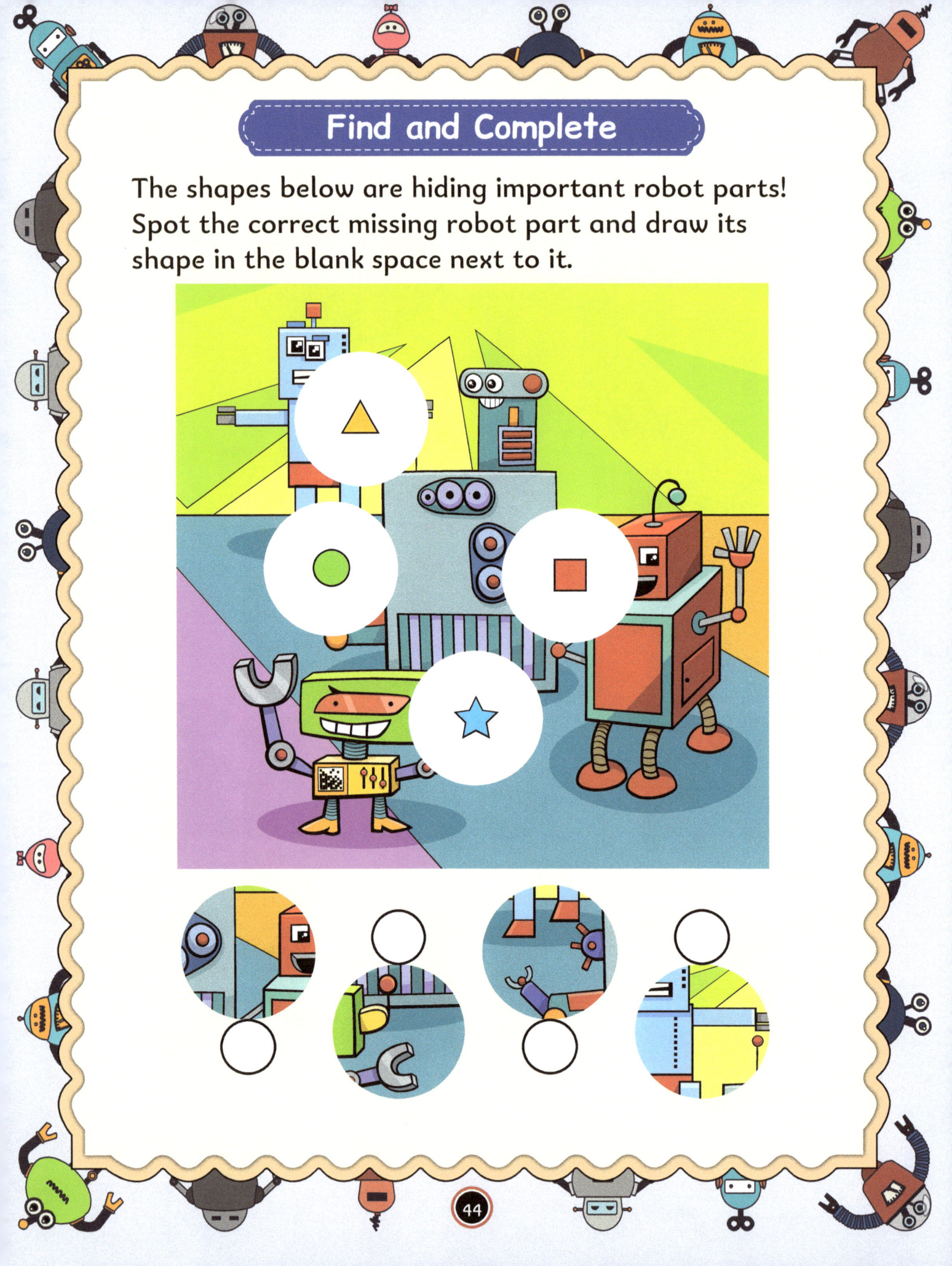

Robot Quiz!

1. What is a robot?
   a) A human with special powers
   b) A machine that can do tasks automatically
   c) A type of animal
   d) A piece of furniture

2. Which of these is NOT a job a robot might do?
   a) Cooking food
   b) Cleaning floors
   c) Playing sports
   d) Reading books out loud

3. True or False: Robots can think and make decisions just like humans.
   ___ True
   ___ False

4. What do robots usually need to work properly?
   a) Food
   b) A remote control
   c) A battery or power source
   d) A pet to take care of

5. Fill in the blank: Robots are used in factories to _____ cars.

6. What does a robot's "sensor" do?
   a) Makes it dance
   b) Helps it see or feel things around it
   c) Powers up the robot
   d) Helps it talk to humans

7. Which of the following is a famous robot from a movie?
   a) Wall-E
   b) Bumblebee
   c) R2-D2
   d) All of the above

8. True or False: Robots can only work inside factories and cannot help at home.
   ___ True
   ___ False

9. Fill in the blank: In the future, robots might help us with _____ (e.g., cooking, studying, cleaning).

10. What do we call robots that can look and move like animals?
    a) Animalbots
    b) Roboanimals
    c) Biomimicry robots
    d) Pet bots

11. How do robots in space explore planets?
    a) They talk to aliens
    b) They walk around with humans
    c) They collect rocks and take pictures
    d) They build houses on other planets

12. True or False: A robot can never be controlled by a human.
    ___ True
    ___ False